The Life and Work of...

Auguste Rodin

Richard Tames

Heinemann Library
Chicago, Illinois

© 2001 Reed Educational & Professional Publishing
Published by Heinemann Library,
an imprint of Reed Educational & Professional Publishing,
100 N. LaSalle, Suite 1010
Chicago, IL 60602
Customer Service 888-454-2279
Visit our website at www.heinemannlibrary.com

Designed by Celia Floyd
Originated by Dot Gradations
Printed in Hong Kong/China

05 04 03 02 01
10 9 8 7 6 5 4 3 2 1

Library of Congress Cataloging-in-Publication Data
Tames, Richard.
    Auguste Rodin / Richard Tames.
      p. cm. – (The Life and work of--)
    Includes bibliographical references and index.
    Summary: Briefly examines the life and work of the French sculptor, describing and giving examples of his art.
    ISBN 1-57572-342-5
    1. Rodin, Auguste, 1840-1917—Juvenile literature. 2. Sculptors—France—Biography—Juvenile literature. [1. Rodin, Auguste, 1840-1917. 2. Sculptors. 3. Art appreciation.] I. Title. II. Series.

NB553.R7 T34 2000
730'.92—dc21
[B]   00-025786

Acknowledgments
The Publishers would like to thank the following for permission to reproduce photographs:

Bridgeman Art Library/Musée d'Orsay, Paris, p. 21; Musée Rodin, Paris, pp. 4, 6, 14, 20, Hélène Moulonguet, p. 7; Adam Rzepka, pp. 5, 9, 13, 18, 25; Charles Aubry, pp. 10, 12; Erik and Petra Hesmerg, p. 11; Bruno Jarret, p.15; Jessie Lipscomb, p.16; Jêrome Manoukian, pp.17, 23; Pierre Bonnard, p. 22; Edward Steichen, p. 24; Choumoff, p. 28; Jean de Calan, p. 29; Photo RMN/R. G. Ojeda, p. 19; Roger-Viollet/Harlingue-Viollet, p. 26; Trip/Christopher Rennie, p. 27

Cover photograph reproduced with permission of AKG London

Some words are shown in bold, **like this.** You can find out what they mean by looking in the glossary.

Contents

Who Was Auguste Rodin?

Auguste Rodin was a French artist and **sculptor**. He is most famous for his **statues** of people. His statues were made of clay, **bronze,** and **marble**.

Auguste tried to show feelings in his **sculptures**. The people in this sculpture are unhappy. Their city in France has been taken over by an English king.

Early Years

Auguste was born in Paris, France on November 12, 1840. Here is a photograph of Auguste with his mother. He was nine years old. He started drawing when he was ten.

Auguste went to a special drawing school when he was fourteen. He began to make clay models at fifteen. His **sculptures** were based on his drawings of people.

Hard Times

Auguste began to earn money by making stone decorations for buildings. When his sister died in 1862, he was very sad. He tried to become a **monk**. But he soon returned to his work.

Sometimes Auguste worked for other people in the day. Then he worked on his own models in the evening. When he was nineteen, he made this head of his father.

Great Changes

In 1864, when he was 24, Auguste got his first **studio**. He also met Rose Beuret. She became his lifelong helper.

Auguste made this **bust** of a young woman the year after he met Rose. It is called *Young Woman in a Flowered Hat.*

Leaving Paris

To earn money, Auguste worked in Belgium from 1871 to 1875. Then he went to Italy for a year. He studied the work of the **sculptor** Michelangelo.

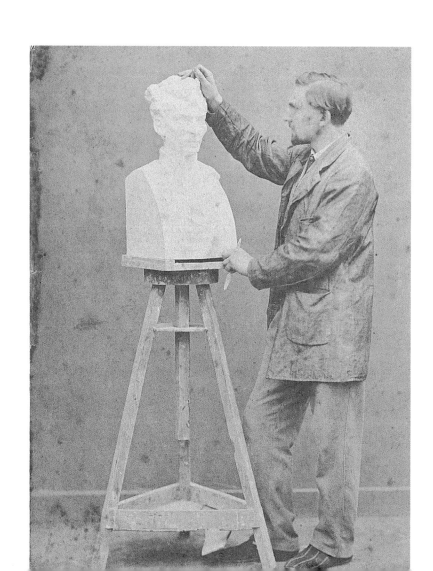

Auguste wanted to show his sculpture, *Man with the Broken Nose,* at an important **exhibition**. But it was turned down. Many people did not like Auguste's **realistic style**.

Fame at Last

Auguste had to wait until he was almost 40 to become famous. His life-size **statue** of a soldier, which he called *Age of Bronze,* brought him fame—and problems, too.

Some people thought Auguste cheated. They thought he made the *Age of Bronze* from **casts** of a real person. They did not believe that Auguste could create such a real-looking figure.

The Work of a Lifetime

In 1880, Auguste began making a huge doorway. It was for a Paris museum. The ideas for his drawings and plans came from a poem by an Italian poet named Dante.

Auguste's most famous **statue**, *The Thinker*, is supposed to be Dante. It was supposed to go on the top of the doorway.

Camille

This **bust** of Auguste was made by **sculptor** Camille Claudel in 1888. Auguste liked the bust very much. Camille helped Rodin with his work. She also **posed** for him.

Camille posed for this **sculpture**. It is called *Thought,* and Auguste made it in 1888. In it, Camille wears a hat usually worn by brides in northern France.

A Big Studio

Auguste moved to Meudon, near Paris. Here he had a big, new **studio.** He often had up to 50 helpers there. They made **carvings** from his clay models.

Rodin loved to read. He got many ideas from books. In 1897, he made this **bust** of a great French writer named Victor Hugo.

Famous Faces

Auguste made **busts** of his friends and people he wanted to thank. Here he makes a bust of French **sculptor** Jean Alexandre Falguière.

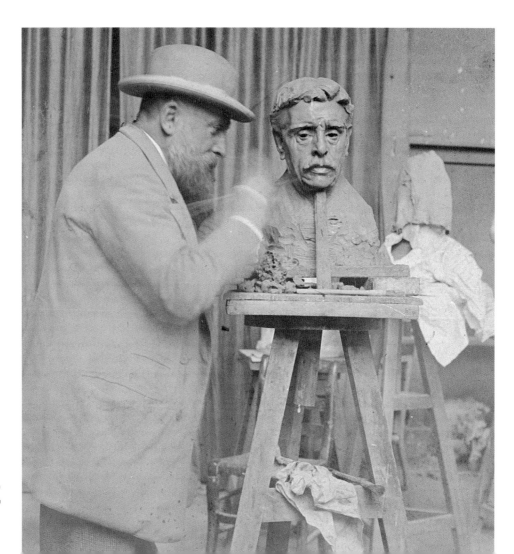

Auguste showed this **statue** of French writer Honoré de Balzac at an **exhibition** in 1898. Auguste had read Balzac's books.

Success

In 1900, Auguste had his first big **exhibition** in Paris. It included over 150 of his **sculptures**. People came from all over the world to see his work.

Auguste called this sculpture *The **Cathedral**.* He thought that the two hands raised together looked like the pointed arches in cathedrals.

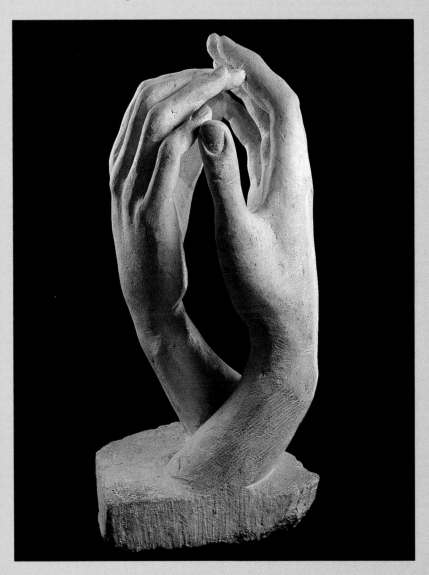

Home and Museum

In 1903, German poet Rainer Maria Rilke wrote a **biography** about Rodin. This picture shows Rainer with Rose and Auguste and their dogs. They stand outside their house at Meudon.

Rainer invited Auguste to the Hotel Biron in Paris. This building became Auguste's home. Today, it is the Rodin Museum. People come here to see his best work.

Last Days

Auguste married Rose in January of 1917. Only two weeks later, she died. He died on November 17, 1917. They were buried together at Meudon under a copy of Auguste's **statue** of *The Thinker.*

When Rodin died, the great doorway he had been working on was left unfinished. It can be seen at the Rodin Museum in Paris.

Timeline

1840	René-François-Auguste Rodin born on November 12
1854	Enters drawing school
1862–1863	Tries to become a **monk**
1864	Meets Rose Beuret
1870	Joins the army
1871	Leaves the army and moves to Belgium
1875–1876	Travels in Italy to study art
1877	Moves back to Paris
1880	Is asked to make the great doorway for museum
1897	Moves to Meudon
1900	Shows 150 sculptures at a Paris **exhibition**
1903	Rainer Maria Rilke writes Auguste's **biography**
1914	Auguste publishes book on **cathedrals** of France
1917	Auguste dies, November 17

Glossary

biography   story of a person's life

bronze   metal made of tin and copper

bust   statue of a head and shoulders

carving   object cut out of wood or rock

cast   form made by putting liquid plaster on a person, letting it harden, taking it off the person, and pouring hot metal in to make a statue

cathedral   large church

exhibition   show of works of art in public

marble   special kind of limestone rock

Michelangelo   famous artist who lived in the 1400s

monk   man who devotes his life to religion

pose   to stand or sit in a certain way while someone paints or draws you

realistic style   way an artist makes things look life-like

sculptor   person who makes statues or carvings

sculpture   statue or carving

statue   carved, molded, or sculpted figure

studio   room or building where an artist works

More Books to Read

An older reader can help you with these books.

Burby, Liza. N. *A Day in the Life of a Sculptor.* New York: Rosen Publishing Group, Inc., 1999 .

Scholastic, Inc. Staff. *The Art of Sculpture: Stone, Wood, Plaster, & Bronze: from Small Statuettes to Cathedrals.* New York: Scholastic, Incorporated, 1995.

More Artwork to See

Bust of a Young Girl, The National Gallery of Art, Washington, D.C.

The Kiss, San Francisco Museum of Fine Arts, San Francisco, California

Sister and Brother, Indianapolis Museum of Art, Indianapolis, Indiana

The Thinker, Detroit Institute of Arts, Detroit, Michigan

Index